NED VENTURES

Teenage Life In The 1950s

Written by

Edward Allan Faine

Happy Ventures!

IM Press

First Printing 2001
Manufactured in the United States of America

IM Press
P.O. Box 5346
Takoma Park, Maryland 20913-5346
301-587-1202
efaine@yahoo.com

Cover design by Joan C. Waites.
All rights reserved by artist.

Front cover and interior photos provided by :
From Out Of the Past Books of Alexandria, Virginia 703-768-7827

Back cover "Slam Book" photo by Gerald A. Consalvi

Some of these stories appeared in different form in New England Writers Network, Raconteur , Slice of Life, and Sweet Annie Review: *Olden Times.*

Library of Congress Cataloging-in-Publication Data

Faine, Edward Allan, 1937-
Ned ventures: teenage Life in the 1950s/written by Edward Allan Faine
p. cm.
Summary: Ned experiences the highs and lows of being in high school in the 1950s.
ISBN: 0-9654651-7-9
[1. High schools—Fiction. 2. Schools—Fiction] I. Title

PZ7.F1436 Ng 2001
[Fic]—dc21

00-033423

See last page 64 for ordering and other information.

CONTENTS

THE BIKE RACE

The bike race was two days away, and I was worried. I couldn't beat old snot-mouth Neal, I told Pudge, two times, but he wouldn't listen. Yeah, sure, Pudge was my best friend and all, but sometimes he did things I just didn't understand. He told me, "Ned, it's for your own good," sounding for all the world like my mother. I tried to get out of the race, but he wouldn't hear of it.

Sometimes I felt he did things for me because I didn't have a father, always saying he would look after me, and all because he was fourteen, six months older than me. But, hey, having Pudge for a best friend was better than having an orange crush at Doc's Drugstore everyday after school; better than having season tickets at old Memorial Stadium right behind the Indians dugout; and better than having one of those newfangled television sets all to yourself in your own house. But a bike race with Neal?

Pudge had set up the race on his own, telling everybody I could whip Neal hands down. Nobody believed it, of course; that's why they were all coming to the vacant field beneath the Triskett overpass on Saturday afternoon. I could just see Pudge, looking like one of those movie star kids, charming the pants off Carole Clark and Nancy Harkness. He'd be smiling ear to ear, all animated and the like, sweeping his hand through his tousled blonde hair. Because I was his best friend, both Carole and Nancy would come up to me in school, never together, of course, and tell me how cute he was—Yeeks, how I hated that word *cute*—and how they loved his freckles, and his sunny disposition, and how they thought he would grow up to be taller than Perry Como, and better looking. They'd ask me all kinds of personal questions about Pudge: Did he really lift weights everyday after school? Did he really send away for the *Charles Atlas* bodybuilding course? Did he die his hair in the summertime, or were those blonde streaks natural? And how come he didn't taper his Levi pant legs like some other guys? Said they needed stuff for their slam books, promised they'd put nice things in their books about me, too. Said Pudge and I were so popular we were the only boys at Marshall High to have a separate slam book. I could care less. They drove me nuts asking me what *he* said about them. Carole and Nancy would come to the bike race, that's for sure, not to see Neal cross the finish line an hour before me, but to see Pudge.

Funny about those two, best friends, but different as snowflakes. Carole was the pretty one, with a killer smile and silky blonde hair, and a shapely figure like a model; looked like she belonged in senior high. The older guys at Marshall High were all the time hanging around her, which four-eyed Nancy probably thought it was because of her. Okay, Nancy wasn't all that bad looking; she was shorter with wavy brunette hair that fell to her shoulders. She reminded me of a school marm in a western. Carole and Nancy dressed alike everyday at school: pleated blue skirts with white blouses and saddle shoes one day, yellow cashmere sweaters with plaid skirts and penny loafers the next. And if you get Carole and Nancy to show up, you just might as well invite their giggly-wiggly girl friends, Linda, Laura, and Bonnie, although I hoped Bonnie wouldn't bring her boyfriend Brad, who pushed me around in gym class, along with that ape Bluto—him I didn't want to see at all.

Of course, Chalky would come. He loved being at the center of things, especially in a crowd. Always the joker he could dance already—a regular Italian Mickey Rooney. He was the first in our class to wear the new fluorescent colors: chartreuse gabardine slacks with a shocking pink shirt. Whew!

Everybody called him Chalky because he had this Italian name with so many "c's" and "i's" in it, nobody could pronounce it, let alone spell it. Nancy hinted several times to me that the girls she knew at Marshall High didn't have good things to say about him in their slam books. He kidded people a lot, had that Italian olive skin, with natural shiny black hair that didn't need Bandoline to hold it in place. He'd probably grow up to look like Frankie Sinatra. Yeah, too jokey, that was his problem. But a nice kid, don't get me wrong.

My second best friend Ralph would be there, too. Ralph was like me, slight-built and sort of shy. He didn't stick out, just a regular guy. I don't think anybody could describe either one of us—we were American looking, no curly hair or big noses or anything like that. We didn't have bulging muscles or freckles or big smiles, you know, regular looking. We looked a touch scrawny, well no, as Mother put it, slight-built, that's why the apes in gym class pushed us around from time to time. But I could run like the roadrunner, made the seventh grade track team, but it didn't mean I could bike faster than Neal.

Neal would flatten me in the bike race, mostly because he had an English racer, the first anyone had seen on the west side of Cleveland. He got it from an uncle who had been to England. It was beautiful. Sleek. Thin tires. Gears. Neal raised the seat so that he looked like one of those old time big-wheeled bikers. He worked on the bike every night, cleaning the gears, oiling them, adjusting the spokes, telling you everything he did the next day, whether you wanted to hear it or not. The bike was beautiful.

Neal himself was ugly, not his looks so much, but they way he acted. Big mouth ugly. How he got away with the things he said, I'll never know. Maybe because he was solidly built, not a big bruiser like Brad or stupid Bluto, but tall, muscular, athletic, and he knew it. Knew he was handsome, too, told you all the time. But that didn't mean the girls liked him. No way. They called him conceited, stuck-up, smart britches. He even tapered his Levi pant legs—said they were "pegged"—and wore tight knit sweaters, and claimed he did it to improve his bike speed, it didn't matter to the girls though. I can't imagine what they wrote in their slam books about him. They never told you because they weren't supposed to.

Big mouth Neal followed me around saying nasty things, although he toned it down in front of Pudge. He was in the gang with Pudge, Chalky, Ralph and me because he lived in our neighborhood off West 140th street—geography is everything. Yeah, old Neal hit home runs, and had that bike. That beautiful bike. That beautiful bike that was going to leave me in the dust on Saturday, with show-off Neal riding high on that pointy English seat, hands off the handlebars, arms outstretched, and me trudging behind on my clunky, one gear, fat-wheeled All-American Schwinn.

As planned, we gathered under the Triskett overpass on Saturday afternoon at one o'clock. Everybody was there, and not just the guys in our gang either, the entire seventh grade class showed up. Most kids had brought their bikes to follow us around the race course. The throng, anxious to get the race underway, started ringing their bike bells. Chalky, no surprise, was the first to start the ribbing. He shouted above the din: "I'm taking bets. Ned wins, I buy you four orange crushes. Neal wins, you buy me one." No takers.

Neal raised up on his bike like he was Roy Rogers on his horse, Trigger, faked a whinney, and sang out: "Now, Chalky is one smart fellow. He knows who's going to win this race."

"I'm betting on the bike, Neal," Chalky said. "Tell you the truth though, I'm gonna have to make the deal sweeter to get someone to bet on Ned. Four orange crushes and a rootbeer milkshake."

Pudge spoke up. "I'll take that bet Chalky." Deathly quiet. Everybody, including me, looked at Pudge like he had admitted to drowning his goldfish. He had to be crazy. I rang my bell, trying to get Pudge's attention. It was bad enough that I was going to embarrass myself in front of everybody, but Pudge didn't have to lose a dollar on my account.

Chalky leaped in the air. "Paisano, you're on. Let's get started."

Pudge called for order as everybody crowded around him, Carole on one side, Nancy, the other. "Here are the rules, you start at Triskett and 140th, go down Triskett to Warren Road, cut down Warren to Lakewood Heights, then over to 140th again and cut back here by way of my house, through my driveway across this here field," gesturing to the tall grassy open space in front of us, "following the path that leads to this spot."

Pudge raised his voice. "And remember, those of you who are going to tag along, don't get in front of the racers."

Neal, chin in the air, piped up. "You mean don't get in front of Ned, I'll be long gone."

Pudge led the group to the corner of 140th and Triskett, raised a red bandana and waved it about.

Amid shouts of excited yelps directed mostly at me, Pudge finally barked out: "You're at the starting gate, gentlemen, may the best bike win... you're off."

I jumped on my bike and pedalled away, shaking my head, thinking Pudge is off his rocker. I looked around. Neal was nowhere in sight. He had laid back, obviously giving me a headstart. Great, I'll finish ten mintues after Neal, instead of fifteen.

I swung my bike out on Triskett Road to make better time off the sidewalk. I craned my neck around, and, sure enough, I spotted a swarm of bees chasing a fleeing beekeeper as Neal and his biking entourage contined their steady advance. I wondered when Neal would make his move and sweep by me laughing. I veered right on Warren Road, pedalling away on the fast track, in the street, but swinging up on the sidewalk during open, smooth stretches. I knew the neighborhood better than Neal. I'd biked it more often than he did—my only real advantage.

At Lakewood Heights Boulevard, where the rich people had their stately houses and large green manicured lawns, I switched to the smooth, wide sidewalk. I wouldn't make better time, but it would be easier biking, and save my energy for the stretch back up 140th street. That's where I expected Neal to catch up and pass me.

I could hear the biking menagerie coming up from behind, and then, as expected, swoosh, Neal darted in front of me. He slowed down, til I caught up with him. "Thought you had a chance, didn't you, Neddy boy. Even with a headstart you don't have a prayer. Just watch me burn up 140th, top gear all the way to the finish line without breaking a sweat. With you still out here on 140th chug-chugging on that balloon-tired bike."

Neal chortled. "Just listen to my tires whistle. The

sound of speed." He loved to torment me. He yelled back over his shoulder, "Did I ever tell you how light my bike is? I can lift it with one finger. It's made of the lightest metal known to man. They use it on jet airplanes. I bet you can't even lift that monstrosity you're riding. What's it made of? Lead?" He chortled again and sped off.

Well, I had no choice now but to keep grinding away and cross the finish line no more than ten minutes after Neal. I had to forget about my sore tired legs, keep my concentration, and ignore those crazy kids behind me, although I could hear Ralph yelling encouragement. I looked ahead and spied Neal spinning away, becoming smaller and smaller by the minute. Soon, I lost sight of him altogether.

I reached the street Pudge lived on, and swung into his driveway like he said. I was ahead of the pack of trailing bikers by a block or so. At least I'd beat them.

I bumped onto the sandy path to cross the field to the Triskett overpass and the finish line. The going was rough over an inch of soft sand on top of a rock bumpy path. They had probably cut the path through the field for the heavy duty trucks when they constructed the overpass several years ago. Good thing I had the Schwinn with its big fat tires to ride up and down the crisscrossing ruts. Big fat tires. Big fat tires?!

I wondered how Neal was doing in his thin sliver of a bike. No way he could fly across this rutted path with that sleek English racer. Even if he jumped off the trail, onto the tall grass field, he couldn't make good time. Sure enough, up ahead I saw Neal, maybe a football field away, walking his bike. Walking his bike. Oooh boy!

I bore down, I had a chance, the finish line was maybe three-five minutes away. Neal spotted me and jumped back on his bike, but he tottered back and forth sideways, making little headway. As I passed him, his bike collapsed to the ground, taking him with it.

I saw the finish line up ahead where somebody had tied balloons to the bushes. Pudge, I saw Pudge, pumping his arm up and down, shouting, "Double time. Double time." Carole and Nancy and some other girls were jumping up and down, screaming their guts out. Oh, Pudge, I thought, you son-of-gun, you knew this all along, didn't you. Oh, boy, oh boy... oh boy.

I passed the bush balloons and fell to the ground. Carole and Nancy and the others immediately surrounded me, propping me up so they could pin this award ribbon on my shirt. I stood there in a daze, knees buckling, trying to catch my breath, trying to smile. All I wanted was an ice cold vanilla creme soda. I was parched.

The bike brigade stumbled across the line and joined the knot of kids around me, slapping me on the back, laughing, yelling. You'd have thought the Indians had won the pennant or something. Neal was nowhere in sight.

Pudge put his arm around my shoulders, smiled at me and then grabbed Chalky by the shirttail, "Old man, I'll see you at Doc's Drugstore after school on Monday for my first orange crush."

§ § §

JOHNNY SLIP-UP

I grabbed my notebook, slammed the locker door and headed for homeroom class. I spotted some ninth-graders coming toward me. One looked my way and mocked, "Hey, klutz, whatcha gonna mess up today?"

The others chimed in, "Hold that book tight, butterfingers. Don't drop it on someone," and, "Step aside, guys, he's gonna fall again." They passed by laughing as Neal greeted me next.

"What's up, Neddy-boy? Or should I say, Spasmo?"

"Cool it, Neal, I gotta get to class."

I walked past homeroom, slipped into an empty classroom and sat down. I wondered how I'd screwed up so badly. I didn't deserve the reputation I had.

My friend Ralph stuck his head inside the doorway. "Aren't you coming to homeroom?"

"I don't know," I said wistfully.

Ralph took the seat in front of me and asked, "Why so bummed?"

"It's...it's, you know, it's the ninth-graders calling me a klutz when I'm not. Then again, who knows, maybe I am. I've done some stupid things lately."

"Come on, don't be so hard on yourself. You're faster than spit and the only seventh-grader on the track team."

I shook my head, unable to say a word.

"Hey, you whipped hot dog Neal in the bike race, didn't you."

Pudge set that up, and Ralph knew it, too. I didn't lose the race, that was the good thing, but I sure couldn't take credit for it.

"You're not clumsy at all," Ralph continued. "I'd say you're sort of like a slapstick comic. Kids always laugh at your tricks. Remember that time you burst through the glass door in science class? Man, what an entrance. Exploding into the room in a shower of glass...and no one got hurt."

"I was late for class," I added, hoping he'd understand I didn't do it on purpose.

Excited, he continued. "And remember when you set those birds free in biology class? Man, that was a hoot. It took us the whole period to capture those flying devils."

"I knocked over the cage, Ralph. I didn't set them free on purpose."

"Oh, sure, just like it was an accident when you marked-up old man Wilson."

"I told you, Ralph, I was asking him a question about our homework and, you know how I talk with my hands, well, the pen was in my hand, swipe, I left a mark on his shirt."

"But you did it twice. No way it was an accident."

Annoyed, I said, "Look, Ralph, I've been clumsy at times, that's all there is to it." I grabbed his arm and shook it. "What about the time I knocked myself out in the schoolyard?"

"That was a fluke," Ralph argued. "You fell off the traveler bars and hit your head on the concrete. That doesn't make you a klutz. It could've happened to anybody."

It didn't help to explain. Like most seventh-graders, Ralph believed I did those things for laughs and jokingly called me stumble-bunny. It was different with the ninth-graders. They called me clumsy-goat. And Neal, who chided me every chance he got, called me *Spas* and *Mongo*—short for spastic and mongoloid—just to show kids he knew big words more than anything else.

The school bell rang and we both scurried down the hall to homeroom class. Mrs. Cochran raised her eyebrow when we walked in. "Welcome, Ralph and Ned, glad you could be with us today. Please be so kind as to take a seat.

"Okay, class, it's our turn to put on the safety play. As always, the theme will be A-B-C."

"Always be careful," the class shouted in unison.

"I've chosen a play called *Johnny Slip-Up*. It's about a boy who's always slipping up, falling, and causing accidents. Who wants to play Johnny?"

School marm-in-waiting Nancy Harkness raised her hand first. "It's gotta be Ned." Soon, the whole class shouted my name. I slid further down in my seat and cupped my hands over my ears. It was the last thing I needed. I'd be known as Johnny Slip-Up for the rest of my life.

"It's unanimous," the teacher announced. "Ned is Johnny. Now, let's see, Carole, you're the narrator. Nancy you can be Johnny's classmate. The rest of you with your hands raised—we'll get your parts straight after school. We have a week to practice. The play will be in the auditorium next Thursday at two o'clock."

Every day for the next week the cast practiced for an hour after school. I had the easiest part—no lines. I acted out the part of Johnny while Carole narrated what I should've done to avoid my slip-ups. During rehearsals, I walked through the routines so others could learn their lines, but that was it. Some kids, especially Ralph, wanted me to put more *oomph* into my bits and do them like I did things in real life. I was none too happy about being Johnny.

After the last rehearsal, the entire cast went to Doc's Drugstore for chocolate phosphates. Ralph snapped a commemorative photo of everybody smiling, then most kids left for home. Carole and Nancy nudged me into a booth. They sat on either side of me, squishing me between them. Nancy said, "We're worried the play's going to flop. If you'd only act up like you do in class, then the play'll be a smash."

Carole agreed. "Ned, we know what's bothering you. Are you listening?" I was, but my thoughts were on her silky blonde hair that curled around the blue beret she wore. She went on: "You're afraid everyone will think you're a real slip-up."

"What are you saying?" I responded, raising my voice. "My reputation's at stake here. Some kids think I'm a slip-up already. After the play, everybody will think so. After all, *I got picked for Johnny.*"

"You gotta look at it different," Nancy reasoned. "The better you are as Johnny, the better everyone will think of you as Ned. Everyone will think the crazy things you do in class are for fun, not spastic like Neal says."

"Please, pretty please?" Carole begged. "Do it for us."

Oooh, that got me. Carole purring in my ear like that. I hesitated and then said, "I'll think about it."

"Great! Let's toast our success," Carole said, as we raised our coke glasses. "Break a leg!"

"Huh?"

"No, no, Johnny...I mean, Ned. Don't break a leg for real. It's just what they say opening night on Broadway for good luck."

"Gosh! I thought you meant it. Knowing me, I'd probably do it, too!"

After a sleepless night mulling over my plight, I decided to take the girls' advice and put my thespian heart into the role. I had nothing to lose and, as they said, everything to gain. More important, I'd give Neal and the rest of them their money's worth—I'd play Johnny like a crazy wild-man. I'd pretend I was Charlie Chaplin and be the actor Mother thought I'd grow up to be. I'd probably get in trouble—after all, it was a safety play—but my reputation was more important than some stupid safety rules everybody already knew.

The next afternoon at assembly, the curtains opened to reveal a school room set—desk, table, chairs, wastebasket and chalkboard. Carole began her narration when I entered eating a banana. I threw the peel over my shoulder, sat on a chair and teetered back and forth until I hit the floor. I got up, slammed the chair down on my foot and hobbled around on one leg until I slipped on the banana peel. I was on the floor again. The auditorium grew quiet. I jumped up to applause, checked the smiling cast in the wings, and went into the next routine. So far, I had followed the script, except for slamming the chair on my foot.

As an example of how *not* to shut the transome or reset the school wall clock, I stacked two chairs on top of a table and climbed to the top. The makeshift ladder toppled, taking me along with it. The audience gasped. I bounced back up and the audience cheered. Carole and the others who stood in the wings stared wild-eyed at me. They hadn't seen me pile two chairs on top of the table in rehearsal.

Carole continued her narration and I promptly slipped on the banana peel again. Jerry Lewis couldn't have done it better.

The next segment featured one staged screw-up after another. I pretended to cut myself with a pocket knife and to get a sliver in my finger from an old board. I knocked people over and poked them with stage scissors more times than called for in the script.

The students roared as if they were watching the *Three Stooges* instead of a safety play. Kids in the wings were mouthing in stage whispers: "Slow down!" "Follow the script!" I heard them, but it was the audience that mattered, not some silly old script.

In the match safety scene, I set fire to paper in the wastebasket. Amidst howls of laughter, a stagehand sprinted on stage and squelched the fire with a bucket of water.

The bicycle safety segment didn't exactly follow the script, either. I zigzagged around stage, knocked over props and dumped Ralph, my handle-bar rider off the stage. Carole followed my antics as best she could, but her voice was barely audible above the clamour of the crowd.

The audience screamed so loud during the playground safety scene that they drowned out her narration all together. In the final routine, I had no choice but to follow script. The slip-up occurred off-stage—Johnny is hit by a car after disobeying the traffic patrol boy. Accompanied by the entire cast and wrapped in bandages, I returned to center-stage on crutches. The audience cheered loudly as I improvised one final collapse, falling to the floor as the curtain closed.

Nancy grabbed me first. "What happened? You were supposed to spark it up, not go crazy. You threw everybody off, we all screwed up our parts."

"Listen to them out there," I said. "They loved it. They're still howling."

"Sure they're howling," Carole said angrily. "You turned a safety play into a comedy. They didn't hear half of what I said."

Mrs. Cochran stormed through the wings straight

toward me. "What was the meaning of that performance? That's not how we rehearsed it. The idea! This was supposed to be a safety play." She shook her finger right in my face. "As far as I'm concerned, you'll never be in a school play again. The idea of setting fire to a wastebasket is outrageous. I almost stopped the play right then and there, but I didn't because of the hard work the others had put into the production."

She turned her back to me, then swirled around, hands on hips, and barked, "And where do you think Ralph is? Huh? The dispensary nurse is taking him to the hospital right now. I just hope his nose isn't broken. And you better hope so, too.

"Now I understand why the class picked you for the part—you're a genuine Johnny Slip-Up. You'll see the Principal tomorrow about this."

I slinked off stage. My plan backfired. I upset everybody. The teacher called me a *genuine* Johnny Slip-Up. Worse, I'd hurt poor Ralph. I'd be known as Johnny Slip-Up forever. And I deserved it, too.

After school, I went to the hospital and waited while they tended to Ralph. I hadn't counted on hurting anyone. I figured if anyone got hurt it would be me. But somebody else? It hadn't entered my mind.

My spirits lifted when Ralph walked into the waiting room accompanied by his mother. His nose was bandaged but it didn't cover his smile. Ralph pulled me aside and confided, "Forget about it. My nose hurts, but it's not broken. I'll be okay in a week." And then he added with a laugh, "Don't worry, we're still friends, even though everybody'll call you Johnny Slip-Up."

Lucky for me, though, it didn't turn out that way.

The next day at school I was a celebrity. Carole and Nancy forgave me, especially after everybody raved about the play. Kids compared me to all three of the *Three Stooges*. Everywhere I turned, somebody congratulated me on my super-dandy performance. Everybody, that is, except the Principal, who threatened to expel me from school. Instead, he gave me an after-school assignment where I had to write *I will always be careful* on the blackboard a thousand times.

While I felt bad about hurting Ralph and mocking safety and upsetting my teacher and cast-mates, I wasn't all that upset with myself. Kids called me Johnny, *not Johnny Slip-Up*. The ninth-graders still made fun of me, calling me a klutz and stuff, but not the same way as before—more like *fun* kidding than *mean* kidding. And Neal didn't call me *Spas* and *Mongo* anymore; it was Neddy-boy or just plain Johnny.

And that was okay with me.

§ § §

A CHRISTMAS LESSON

"Attention, class," Mrs. Cochran announced as she entered the room. "It's Christmas time again. Do you want to put on a play?"

"No," we shouted in unison.

Chalky spun around in his seat, looked at me, and whispered, "Hey Ned, wanna bet she's gonna take us to hear that longhair music again?"

Before I had a chance to answer, Mrs. Cochran said, "Okay, do you want to go to Severence Music Hall?"

A loud *no* resounded throughout the room.

School marm Nancy, always the first to raise her hand, suggested, "Why don't we have a party? Mr. Watson's homeroom class is having one."

Chalky yelled, "Yeah, let's have a party. Tubby can be Santa Claus and give out presents."

Shouts of approval rang out as Mrs. Cochran demanded quiet. "All right, then. But exactly what will we do at a party? Somebody tell me. Nancy, you had your hand up."

"We could bring popcorn balls and grape punch. Decorate a tree and play Christmas records."

"Not *just* Christmas records," I interjected, "Pop records, too. Nat King Cole. Jo Stafford."

Chalky leaped up from his desk. "How about my *goombahs*: Tony Bennett. Rosemary Clooney. He burst into song: "Come on a my house. Come on a, come on."

"Sit down, Chalky. Calm down," Mrs. Cochran

said.

I pinched Chalky in the butt and whispered. "If we're going to have a tree, we gotta have a Santa Claus.

Chalky shouted out: "Tubby for Santa Claus."

"Shut up, Chalky," Tubby growled.

"What about exchanging presents?" Mrs. Cochran asked. "It would be in keeping with the Christmas spirit, wouldn't it?"

Nancy asked, "Can we exchange with whoever we want to?"

The teacher shook her head. "No, we have to be sure everyone gets a present. Let's see, how shall we do it? We'll keep it simple. Exchange with the person in the seat across from you. Rows one and two, three and four, you got it." My heart sank. Across from me sat Stinky Jimmy.

Of all the luck! On the one day when it really mattered, I end up sitting next to Stinky. Served me right for being late to homeroom. Well, I could just forget about getting a decent gift from him.

No one sat next to him on purpose—they couldn't stand the smell. He lived with his father in a shack under the Hilliard Avenue bridge next to a dump. And that's what he smelled like—a smoky, moldy garbage dump. He looked even worse with his smudged hands and face, and half-spiked, half-matted hair. He wore dirty, oversized work pants held up by a long khaki belt, and a randy grey sweater over a short-sleeve shirt, even in the dead of winter. Some kids said he had lice but I never saw any. He was nice enough, though, not pushy like some guys. He smiled when he passed you in the hall, but that worked to his disadvantage. His teeth looked rotten. He didn't have any friends and kept to himself. I often wondered why he seemed so happy.

The bell rang and the gang gathered in the hall next

to Chalky's locker where he was holding court as usual. "Ain't I lucky? Carole is going to give me a present."

"Yeah," Pudge seconded, "But what are you going to give her?"

"I'll get her a fuzzy cashmere sweater a size too small," Chalky bragged.

"I wish I was as lucky as you," Pudge lamented, "I got stuck with hoity-toity Eloise. She'll probably give me a hanky 'cause she's all the time telling me to cover my nose when I sneeze."

"What are you going to get her?" Chalky asked.

"A Brillo pad to scour her braces."

Everybody laughed and Pudge asked Ralph what he was going to get Tubby. "A wheelbarrow to carry his lunch in."

Chalky roared and then looked at me. "Hey, Ned, who did you get."

"Stinky."

"You've gotta be kidding," Chalky said, slapping the locker loudly with his open hand. "Bet you're gonna get a half-eaten fish wrapped in an old newspaper."

"Whaddya gonna give him?" Ralph asked.

"A bath," I said.

Everybody chuckled as we sauntered down the hall to our next class. Waiting for me on the stairwell landing, Stinky smiled and said, "I'm gonna get you something you'll really like."

"Thanks but I gotta get to science class," I said, rushing past him up the stairs.

After class I bumped into him in the hall. "Uh, Stink...I mean Jimmy. I gotta go."

I couldn't let Stinky follow me around. I'd have to find a way to shake him. The smell I could stand. But what would people think if they saw me hanging around *him*?

Two weeks later I still hadn't gotten him a gift. Picking a present for somebody who didn't have much was difficult. I couldn't ask anybody in class what to get him because nobody really knew him. And I couldn't ask *him* what he wanted. I knew he wanted to make friends, but I didn't want to be seen with him—otherwise I'd be shunned, too.

The day before the party, I went to Doc's Drugstore and bought a pencil set. He already had pencils but so what.

The next day I rushed into the room, threw the present under the tree, and joined the gang in the corner. I avoided Stinky's gaze coming from the other side of the room where he sat alone. Nancy and Eloise circled the room and offered everyone home-baked cookies. Other kids sorted through stacks of records. The gang talked excitedly about the upcoming holidays and joked about the gift exchange.

"Did you get Carole a sweater, Chalky?"

"Naw. Got her something better. A gym suit covered with itchy powder. Just wait to you see her on the playground this spring."

"Ah, c'mon, tell us what you really got her?" Pudge tweaked.

"Not gonna tell you. You'll find out soon enough," Chalky replied.

"Don't say anything," Ralph whispered. "But I got Tubby a jump rope."

"Come on, you didn't," Pudge said sternly, "he'll hate you for that. You should've got him a real gift."

"Shhh, I was just kidding," Ralph said between his teeth. "Besides, Ned's the only one who's gonna get a stupid present. Ain't that right, Ned?"

"Yeah, but I don't care. I didn't get Stinky much, either."

The teacher told us to take our seats for the entertainment. Eloise played her violin, Nancy recited a poem and everybody sang, *Frosty the Snowman*. Then Mrs. Cochran announced it was time to exchange gifts and asked for quiet. "I know you're having fun but we must never forget the true meaning of the Christmas season. I'm glad you wanted to exchange gifts because giving represents the true spirit of Christmas."

She cleared her throat and continued. "You've all heard that it's better to give than to receive. You've also heard that it's the thought—not the gift—that counts. Both are very true.

"Just remember, as you go through life, you'll be marked not by what you receive, but by what you give."

Then she told the row monitors to distribute the gifts. Bedlam followed. Chalky waved the red suspenders he got from Carole. Pudge blew the harmonica Eloise had given him and Ralph flipped the football present from Tubby.

Out of the corner of my eye, I saw Stinky arranging the pencils I'd given him on his desk top.

Everybody turned in their seats as the row monitor walked down the aisle to hand me a five-foot long package wrapped in shiny silver paper with a big red bow. Chalky yelled, "Open it. Open it."

Fascinated, the class looked on while I opened the package. I thought it would be a baseball bat Stinky found at the dump, but the box was labeled *Genuine Red Ryder Air Rifle.* Astonished, I opened the box and removed a brand new air rifle. My classmates eagerly crowded around to get a closer look. It was beautiful and even more striking than its picture on the back cover of those comic books. And as advertised, *Red Ryder* was etched on both sides of the wooden stock. Everybody wanted to hold it but I gave it to Pudge first.

I had wanted a *Red Ryder* B-B gun ever since the

fourth grade. I wondered how Stinky knew. He beamed as girls huddled around and praised him for giving me such a nice gift. The rifle was the hit of the party. Concerned by the commotion, Mrs. Cochran ordered us back to our seats and told me to put the rifle back in the box. We sang *Santa Claus is Coming to Town* and the party ended.

My friends gathered in the schoolyard for another look at the B-B gun. We figured Stinky found it in the dump after some kid's mother threw it away. No way he could afford it. Even so, the gang agreed I got the best present of the day.

Chalky observed, "Boy, did we make out like bandits." He hesitated. "And you know, I should've given Carole a better gift."

"I know what you mean," Pudge said. "I gave Eloise a stupid pot holder. And she gives me a harmonica. If I'd only known."

"Wait, Pudge," Ralph said, "Eloise liked that potholder. She thought the pig picture on it was cute. And Tubby liked the sports book I got him. So everything turned out all right." Ralph turned to me. "Didn't it, Ned?"

"Yeah, sure," I said sheepishly, hoping they wouldn't bring up the pencil set. "Gotta go, guys." I waved good-bye and hurried to the sidewalk. I spotted Stinky waiting for me at the corner.

"See, I told you. I knew you'd like it," he said with a grin a Cheshire cat would be proud of.

"Thanks a lot, Jimmy. It's really super. How'd you know I wanted a *Red Ryder*?" I avoided his gaze and mumbled, "I only wished I'd gotten you something better."

"The pencil set is neat. I can really use them. And they're better than regular school pencils."

"Yeah, well, I should've got you something better."

"I like the pencils fine."

I tucked the box with the air rifle under my arm and stammered, "I'll...I'll walk you...as far as Triskett, but then I gotta get home."

We walked in silence up 140th Street to the bus stop on Triskett Road. I didn't know what to say. Jimmy just smiled. The bus came and I watched him climb aboard the bus and find a seat. He waved at the window. I mouthed, "So long, Jimmy."

What a shame he lived next to a dump. He'd be a member of the gang if he didn't. And what did Mrs. Cochran always say? *You can't tell a book by its cover.* How right she was. Jimmy sure had a stinky cover but the pages inside smelled okay. But what about me? Nice cover, stinky pages.

Then I remembered what else Mrs. Cochran had said: *You're marked not by what you receive, but by what you give.* Jimmy passed Christmas with an *A plus,* while I flunked with a big fat *F.* Next year I'd get my seatmate a better present and maybe—just maybe—I'd get an *A* plus like Jimmy.

§ § §

PAPERBOY

Luck usually didn't run my way. But when Neal called and offered me his paper route, I wondered if my fortunes were about to change. Although, given that it was Neal, I was a bit hesitant.

"C'mon, Neddy boy," Neal pleaded, "delivering the *West Side News* is no big deal. It's only ten pages, once a week. You just roll it up, slip a rubberband around it, and throw it on people's doorsteps. And you can deliver any time you want on Thursday—morning, noon or night."

"Well, Neal—" I started to say.

"Pudge told me to offer the route to you first. Said it was a real winner.

"And...and don't tell anybody I told you this...but you can miss some houses from time to time and nobody complains. Come on, you should lick this up faster than a fudgecicle in August."

If Pudge thinks it's okay, I thought, what do I have to lose. "Okay, Neal. I'll take it."

A week later, the *West Side News* lady knocked on the door and inducted me into her "paperboy corps" with Mother looking on, smiling. She handed me a canvas bag with thick straps and sternly announced, "This is your newsbag, treat it with respect. And treat your customers with respect, too."

I managed a "Yes, ma'am," but my thoughts were on the easy money. With one day's work I'd make as much loot as kids who had daily paper routes. Quite a coup for a guy whose luck usually ran to the other side of good. Maybe this time Lady Luck would keep on smiling, even if I messed up, which I had a tendency to do from time to time.

I breezed the first two weeks. But in a month or so I got bored silly walking past the same five hundred houses every week, up West 140th Street, then back. Down Lakewood Heights Boulevard, then back; it was almost as boring as those long, numbing car drives with Mother to visit relatives. Like Neal, I cheated every now and then, skipping a few houses, and sometimes a whole block. Anything to shorten the route and relieve the monotony. At first, I stacked the undelivered papers in the basement, but when the pile reached the window, I discarded them in a dump hole in the field behind my house. And just like Neal had said, nobody complained when papers weren't delivered.

One Thursday, as I trudged along the boulevard with my bulging newsbag slung over my shoulder, a light bulb clicked on in my head. Maybe I didn't have to deliver the paper at all. I never saw anybody read the stupid thing. And no wonder, no headlines, sports, or comics like *The Cleveland Plain Dealer*. How could you follow the Indians? Or see what's doing with the Schmoo's in Dogpatch? My mind was made up. The next week, I chucked that week's edition in the dump hole.

The week after, I delivered as usual and, except for one old guy who gave me the dirty eye, everything went hunky-dory. Then I skipped another week. I continued my off-on weekly delivery pattern for the next month. I was living somewhere above cloud nine. All that money and hardly any work. Mother was happy that she didn't have to pay me an allowance, and was looking forward to the day when I would pay room and board. Lady Luck just kept on smiling, so I skipped delivery two weeks in a row to see what would happen.

One evening, Mother opened the door to a stiff *West Side News* lady. "May I speak to Ned?"

"Most certainly. He's right here," Mother indicated, pointing in my direction.

The *News* lady looked passed Mother squarely in my face. "Turn in your newsbag. You're fired!"

"Fired?" Mother gasped. "What in heaven's name for?"

"For not delivering the *West Side News* to his customers like he was supposed to."

"There must be some mistake." Mother turned to me. "Ned, you couldn't have done such a thing... could you?"

I didn't say anything.

"Excuse me. But if you and your son will follow me, I'll show you exactly where Ned's last two months of the the *West Side News* are."

"Yes, I'd like to see what you're talking about." Mother grabbed my arm and tugged. "Come along, Ned."

We stood at the dump site and surveyed the scattered bundles. The *News* lady began her tirade. "Young man, do you have any idea what you've done? Do you know how many older people depend on the *West Side News* for bargains on food, clothes and medicine?" She walked a step away, spun back around and spat out, "Seniors with limited budgets depend on the *News* to live, don't you know."

She settled down somewhat, wiping the spittle from her mouth on her lace glove. She went on in a loud but controlled voice. "People plan their lives around the schedule of meetings and activities in the paper. Handicapped and elderly people depend on it for their special pickups. Others depend on the *News* for the date and time of charitable events that benefit the community.

"You are a disgrace to the paperboy corps. In my ten years with the *West Side News*, we've never had someone so...so...so irresponsible." She faced my mother. "I'm sorry, I thought you should know what your son has done. I hope he will learn a lesson from this."

"Good day," she said smartly and then stormed across the field with my former newsbag slung over her arm.

Mother and I walked silently back to the house, her face ashen, the color of the *News* without the print. Finally, she spoke. "This isn't like you. How could you do such a thing?"

"I'm sorry. I thought the paper was a piece of junk."

"But they paid you to deliver the paper. It didn't matter what you thought."

"You don't have to say anything else, Mother. I should of, you know, stopped and thought about what I was doing."

I went to my room, flopped on the bed and cursed my stupidity. I had finally gotten lucky. Then I went and blew it like a dorky dumbbell. I should've checked with Neal. Hmmm, I thought, he didn't deliver all his papers and he didn't get into any trouble.

I called Neal and told him the whole story.

"You mean," he asked disbelieving, "you trashed the whole bundle? You didn't deliver a one?"

"Yep," I said. "But you got away with it. Didn't you?"

"Gotta away with what?"

"Not delivering the *News* to every house."

"You didn't believe that, did you?" He laughed heartedly. "I told you that so you'd take the route. The darn thing nearly drove me batty. You should've..."

Neal talked on but I didn't hear a word. A fine buddy he turned out to be. I should have known better. Like always, I screwed up and Lady Luck frowned.

Maybe luck wasn't random, something out-of-the-blue like I always thought. Maybe lucky people are the ones who think ahead and do the right thing; it's people who do stupid things—and don't think about the consequences—that are unlucky.

§ § §

THE GREAT KISS

"Hey, Pudge, are we going to play softball tomorrow?" I asked as we turned the corner heading toward Marshall High.

"Yeah, Farmer's Field at six. I gotta get the word out to the guys."

"What's doing at Marshall tonight?"

"Chalky and Neal will be there." Pudge hesitated and then said, "Oh...and some girls."

"Really? Like who?"

"Carole and Nancy." He paused again. "Some others, too."

Why were girls going to be there? I wondered. They never hung out with us guys at Marshall High on summer nights. We shot the breeze—talked baseball and stuff—and planned the next day's adventure. Why would Carole and Nancy be there? Something must be up. I didn't pester Pudge about it. He would've told me if it was important. After all, he was my best friend. Even let me play shortstop and bat fifth on the summer league team even though I was a singles' hitter. I couldn't have asked for a better friend.

As Pudge and I approached Marshall, I spotted swell-head Neal barreling toward us on his bike. He was always after Pudge to put me in right field or lower down in the batting order. Neal wheeled up next to us in his fancy racer (although, after the bike race he hadn't said word one about his fabulous streak machine). "Say Pudge, you still letting Neddy-boy bat fifth? We can't win with him in the middle. You saw him strike out the other day with the bases loaded."

"Yeah, but he also hit a single with a guy on base."

Chalky came up from behind, slapped me on the back and said, "Ned's okay batting fifth for my money. He hit the longest ball I ever saw over at Brook's Field. It didn't go for a homer because it hit a car and bounced back. But it was the longest ever."

Neal muttered, "Accident. Accident," shook his head and sped ahead of us on his bike.

We turned into the Marshall football field and spotted Carole and Nancy sitting in the stands. Chalky yelled to them right away. "Carole Clarke, queen of the dark; Nancy Harkness, queen of the darkness."

"Shut up, Chalky," Carole said, "or I'll tell what people wrote about you in my slam book."

Pudge said, "Tell us. Tell us."

"Well, I can't say exactly. You know the rules. But it sure wasn't good."

"I bet they said worse things about Ned," Neal said.

"Oh, no," Nancy replied. "My book says nothing but nice things about Ned. How shy and cute he is, and how funny he is when he wants to be."

"Yeah, especially when he comes into study hall after gym with his hair all wet and combed back," Carole nodded.

Geez, I thought, is that all girls talk about? How cute I look with my hair combed. It seemed like girls had to say that word *cute* at least a hundred times a day.

"Look at Ned. He's blushing," Carole said.

"No I'm not! And I'm not cute either. If this is all we're going to talk about, I'm going home."

Pudge insisted we all go to Tommy's house. "How's come we're going to Tommy's?" I whispered to Pudge as we walked along a few steps behind the others.

"To see the basement. It's real neat. His dad's a cop and he fixed it up with stuff he got from police raids."

Pudge was right, as always. The basement looked like a movie gangsters' wood-paneled hideout. Tiffany lamps spread soft circles of light next to cushiony sofas scattered about the room. Handcuffs, brass knuckles, and billy clubs hung from studs on the walls. Two pinball machines sat at one end of the basement; a Las Vegas gaming table and a jukebox at the other. Tommy served potato chips and Cokes from his dad's bar. He told us to make as much noise as we wanted. His parents had gone out to a movie and wouldn't be back until midnight.

Other girls showed up. First Laura and Joan, then Linda and Bonnie, but without her boyfriend, Brad. I sure hoped he wouldn't come. He was on the ninth grade wrestling team and bullied me a lot.

The boys took turns playing pinball and roulette, while the girls played the jukebox and danced. Pretty soon everyone but Bonnie paired off—Pudge and Carole in one corner, Neal and Linda in another, Tommy and Joan behind the bar and Chalky in a big chair with Laura. I was left with Nancy, the school marm, on one of the big soft sofas. I couldn't figure out what was going on. It was like everybody decided to play musical chairs, and then somebody blew a whistle and I didn't hear it. "Who's going to start it off?" Carole said.

"You are." Neal replied.

"No, I'm not."

Start off what? I wondered silently.

"I'll do it," Nancy said, leaning over toward me. "I'll give Ned his first kiss." She pushed her lips against mine and held them there for the longest time. I thought I would suffocate. Thank God she pulled away before I exploded.

"How was it, Ned?" Carole yelled from the corner.

"Your first kiss, eh, Neddy-boy?" Neal piped in.

"I've kissed girls before," I lied.

"Like who?"

"Like...I don't remember, there's so many."

Come on, Ned," Carole said, "Own up. If you don't, I'm going to come over and kiss you myself."

Nancy protested, "No, we'll switch later. Right now, Ned's all mine." She leaned over and kissed me again.

If I'd only known this was going to happen, I could've prepared. It was the first time Pudge had let me down. He should've told me. I wondered why he didn't. I was out of breath again. I tickled Nancy, and she broke away.

"What did you do that for?"

"I just wanted to see if you were ticklish."

"I'm your first, ain't I? You can tell me, I won't tell."

"Nope. I kissed girls before."

"Oh, yeah, I bet. Not as good as me, though."

She kissed me again, and I sort of liked it. Maybe Nancy wouldn't grow up to be a school marm afterall. But I just couldn't hold my breath that long. Out of the corner of my eye I saw Neal rolling his head back and forth as he kissed Linda. Chalky and Laura did the same thing. So I rolled my head all the way to one side, opened the corner of my mouth, inhaled, rolled to the other side and exhaled; just like in swimming, except I had to work around Nancy's nose. Thank goodness she had removed her glasses. Just as I mastered the routine, she broke away gasping. "You sure are a long kisser."

I suggested shorter kisses but then she shouted over to Carole, "You want to switch?"

"Okay, I'll be the second girl to kiss Ned."

She kissed me, and it went a little better than with Nancy. Carole rolled her head along with me and varied the pressure of her lips on mine—something Nancy didn't do. When we broke apart, she said in a low voice, but not low enough, "I can tell you've never kissed a girl before tonight."

"Told you so, told you so," Neal crowed.

"Shut up, Neal," Pudge and Chalky yelled in unison.

"He's a better kisser than you are, Neal!" Carole responded. Before she went back to Pudge she leaned over and whispered in my ear, "Pucker up a little bit more and you'll be all right."

It became quiet as a church on a weekday as everybody continued kissing. I thought, kissing can't be all that bad if it keeps girls from talking. But kissing was difficult. There were so many steps to put together. I'd have to practice to get the hang of it.

Nancy pulled away and pouted. "Carol promised me I'd get some time with Pudge, but she's keeping him all to herself. He's the best kisser here, you know."

"No, I don't know. I've only kissed you and Carole."

She laughed, kissed me on the cheek and said, "In a pinch, I guess you'll do," and then she laughed some more.

When everybody was ready to leave, Pudge asked me if I would walk Bonnie home because Brad had never showed up as expected. "Okay, Pudge," I said softly between my teeth, "but you should've told me what was going to happen here tonight."

"You wouldn't have come if I had told you."

He was right, as usual. Looking after me, as always.

Carole bumped up to me, flipped her curly blonde hair with both hands, pulled me to her, and whispered in my ear, "Here's another suggestion, part your mouth a little and rest your tongue on your lower lip."

Great, another tip. I'd just have to practice.

Halfway to her house, Bonnie took hold of my hand. What a night! First, I get kissed and then Bonnie holds my hand. If Brad saw us he'd probably put a headlock on me and squeeze the daylights out of me. I kept an eye out, ready to drop Bonnie's hand in a flash.

When we came to Bonnie's house she said, "Thanks for walking me home, Ned. You're really nice, you know."

She looked at me like she wanted a kiss. With Brad not around, I figured here's my chance to practice. So, I thought, roll the head, inhale, exhale, avoid the nose, vary lip pressure, pucker, part the mouth, stick out the tongue—and kissed her. She pulled back, wide-eyed, and exclaimed, "Tonight's not your first! I bet you've kissed lots of girls before." She looked at the ground, and then said in a whisper, "I wish Brad kissed that good."

"Uh...yeah, well, I've...got to get going. See you Bonnie."

Wow! I'd put it all together, and it was a great kiss. Better than Carole's or Nancy's, and according to Bonnie, better than Brad's.

Maybe I was a singles hitter who should be batting ninth and playing right field instead of shortstop. But with a little practice, I just might become the best kisser around. And then nobody, not even Neal, could say I wasn't.

§ § §

THE PUSHOVER

I hated gym class.

I couldn't climb knotted ropes or tumble on hard floor mats worth a diddley-squit. Gym was for big-boned, tough guys; not slender, wiry guys like me. Most of all, I hated gym because of Bluto—that fat-lipped, brillo-haired, ninth grader who already shaved.

Bluto pushed me around in gym whenever he got the chance. I pretended it didn't hurt and kept quiet. He bullied my friend Ralph, too, but when he complained to the gym teacher, then *everybody* picked on Ralph.

While Bluto was roughing me up, blabber-mouth Neal would tell the world: "How come you let Bluto push you around, Neddy-boy? You his slave, or what?" Neal was in our gang and supposed to be a friend. That didn't stop him from making fun of me, though. I swore I'd get him someday, somehow. But Bluto was my number one problem. Because of him, I had a reputation I couldn't shake—pushover Ned the kids called me. But what could I do?

One day in the cafeteria, Ralph and I sat together at lunch and talked about our common problem. My friend confided, "Bluto's bigger'n us, we can't do anything about him. We'll just have to wait him out. Next year he'll be a tenth-grader and in a different gym class."

"He's so dumb," I lamented, "he probably won't pass and we'll be stuck with him again next year."

"What bums me," Ralph continued angrily, "is that the other seventh-graders stand around and don't say a thing. If we banded together, we could stop him."

"That'll never happen, they're afraid of Bluto. I gotta tell you, I'm so...so..." I slammed the cafeteria table so hard, Ralph's tray jumped and peas rolled off the table. His eyes widened so I said, "Sorry, but...but just yesterday, Nancy Harkness came up to me in that schoolmarmy voice of hers and said, *"I hear they're beating you up in gym. Punch 'em back, Ned, you can do it."* I slouched in my chair and lowered my voice. "Nancy thinks I'm a pushover like the skinny guy in the *Charles Atlas* ad. Maybe I should take the *Atlas* course and kick sand in that bully Bluto's face."

Just as I said that, Bluto snuck up behind and put a choke-hold on me, while another ninth-grader grabbed Ralph and proclaimed, "Well, here they are together, the musclemen of Marshall High."

"They look hungry, heh, heh, like they could do with some mashed potatoes and gravy," Bluto said, pulling my pants back and stuffing mashed potatoes down my rear. The kids at nearby tables roared with laughter, as Bluto loosened his grip and sauntered off smiling. Without thinking I grabbed a stewed tomato from Ralph's tray and heaved it, splattering red goop all over Bluto's face.

Aroused by the commotion, everybody crowded around and whooped and hollered with glee at the sight of smashed tomato all over Bluto's kisser. Not fully realizing what had happened, he stood there stunned for several seconds before he charged at me like an enraged bull. "You little scurve, I'm gonna make you pay for this."

"Pay for what?" Mr. Watson boomed as he threaded his way toward me. Bluto stopped dead in his tracks as Mr. Watson continued, "Stop this noise. Lunch hour is over. Everybody get to your one o'clocks."

Saved from certain death, I went to the lavatory and, with Ralph's help, cleaned the mashed potatoes out of my pants. Shaking like an epilectic in seizure, I missed my one o'clock but recovered in time for my two o'clock Civics class. I entered the classroom to scattered applause. It was the last thing I wanted to hear.

"Way to go," Nancy beamed. "Bluto deserved it. About time somebody stood up to him."

"I...I didn't stand up to him," I stammered, "I just threw a tomato at him. He put mashed potatos down my pants."

"Look," Carole Clarke butted in, "he had it coming. If he tries anything else, you just let me know and I'll get Pudge and the guys to talk to him."

Yeah, sure, I thought, a lot of good that'll do. Nobody, but nobody, ever hit Bluto with anything, much less a tomato. No way Pudge could talk him into forgetting it. Bluto couldn't be reasoned with anymore than a mindless shark. I'd have to face him again, no way around it.

For the next hour I blanked out everything the teacher said and concentrated on my next move. Bluto would be waiting for me after school, I was sure of that. Carole got me to thinking, though. Maybe I could get Pudge and the gang to escort me home. The class bell rang and I dashed out of the classroom and up the middle stairwell. I wanted to get to Pudge fast. Fudge-buns and cement-putty, of all the kids who might have been stairwell monitor that day, there, on the landing, all by himself, was Bluto.

He snatched me and slammed me up against the wall. "You little punk! You scummy little birdbrain! I'm gonna beat you to a pulp. I'll teach you to mess with me," he growled in my face as he squeezed my neck with one hand and twisted my wrist with the other. His face turned red and slobber formed at the corners of his mouth as he threatened, "You're gonna pay...but not here. I'm gonna beat your brains out in front of everybody in the schoolyard. I'll be waiting for you. Bring your tomatoes, twerp." With that he released me and I fell, gasping, to the floor.

I sat there numb. I couldn't move. It wasn't fair. He was almost twice my size. I never fought anybody before. I couldn't beat up somebody like he could, no matter what they did. Bluto had to be avoided, I couldn't walk right into my own funeral. I had to act, fast.

I scampered down to the gym and onto the football field. I walked halfway around the field faking conversation with the cheerleader squad before making a dash for the street. I took a long, roundabout route home to avoid running into kids from Marshall.

Great, just great. Kids at school would think I was a pushover...*and* a coward. Oh, well, at least I still had my ribs. But what would I do tommorow? And the day after that? I couldn't switch schools. I had to face Bluto sometime.

That night I met Pudge in his basement workout weight room. I needed advice. And if he really wanted to take care of me, like he always said he did, now was the time. But he wasn't very sympathetic. "Geez, Ned, you sure know how to pick them. Bluto of all people! He was fuming when you didn't show up after school."

"What am I gonna do? I can't avoid him forever. When he catches me I'm gonna get hurt big time."

"Yeah, I know. He's an animal. Stay away from him as long as you can. Maybe he'll cool down. I'll get some guys to talk to him."

"Thanks," I said, frowning. "Believe me, I'm gonna be the invisible man of Marshall High." I paused for a moment. "Pudge, I've been thinking. You lift weights and all. Maybe you could show me some things, like the *Charles Atlas* dynamic tension stuff." Pudge screwed up his face but I went on. "I'm tired of Bluto kicking sand in my face. I don't want to be a ninety-seven pound weakling all my life."

"Look," Pudge said, putting his arm around my shoulders. "Lifting weights ain't gonna do you no good. You gotta have the right kind of build to begin with, know what I mean? Just forget the *Charles Atlas* course. You gotta play to your strengths." Pudge moved into a fighter's crouch, left arm extended, right hand tucked under his chin and began jogging in place. "You're fast and quick. You gotta stay away from him. Dodge, weave, back-away, run around, anything. Just don't let him corner you. Make him chase you."

"People will think I'm running away."

"Hey, if it works, people will think you're a genius."

"Do I hit him?"

"Sure, not so much to hurt him—I don't think you could anyway—but to get him to chase you. You know, wear him out." He looked me squarely in the eye. "Didya ever see Sugar Ray fight? Fight like that. Whatever you do, don't fight like Slapsie Maxzie or you'll get killed."

"Can we practice? Maybe tonight and...and this weekend?"

"Sure. Let's get started."

It took some doing but I avoided Bluto the next day, sneaking out after lunch and taking the long way home again. I didn't care what people thought; I had the weekend to practice with Pudge.

On Saturday he taught me boxer tricks, like how to avoid getting hit by constantly moving in a circle. On Sunday he taught me to punch, not a cowboy roundhouse like in the movies, but a quick, flicking jab to keep Bluto off balance. We also worked on dirty fighting—biting and kneeing—to help me escape when he caught hold of me.

On Monday, I went to school with a lump in my throat and a growly stomach. Luckily, I didn't see Bluto until lunch time. While I sat at a table with the gang, he just stared at me from the other side of the cafeteria. Pudge reminded me of what we practiced that weekend. I felt safe with my friends around me, that is, until Neal started making noises. "It's a good thing we don't have stewed tomatoes today, otherwise Ned'd be throwing them at everybody. Did you see how he plastered Bluto last week?" Neal looked in Bluto's direction and raised his voice. "And you know what? Bluto didn't do anything about it. Wonder why?"

"Put a lid on it, Neal," Pudge ordered as we got up to leave. We stacked our trays and went out to the corridor while Neal trailed behind. "Bluto's looking for you Neddy-boy. He says you're chicken, afraid to face him for what you did last week."

Pudge snapped, "Neal! Slam it! Keep quiet. How'd you like to have Bluto on your tail?"

"Well, hey, I didn't throw a tomato at him and then run and hide."

"Neal, quit it," I said in a lowered voice, hoping he'd stop talking so loud.

He spied Bluto at the far end of the hall, pointed to me and blared, "Here he is, Bluto. Come and get him."

I didn't know who I was angriest with, Neal or Bluto. But Neal was closer. I let loose an old-fashioned roundhouse to the side of his face, knocking him against the lockers with a bang. The swing caught me, Neal, and everybody by surprise. Time froze. "It's a fight," someone shouted and, suddenly, a throng of noisy, shouting kids surrounded us.

No longer the wiseacre, Neal sprung into action. Steely-faced, teeth clenched, right arm cocked, he edged toward me while kids yelled, "Get him. Get him." Driven by anger, fear, I don't know what and out-of-my-mind, I stormed into him like a madman swinging both arms wildly, every other crazy swing hitting him somewhere on the face. His expression changed from rage to disbelief as a flurry of blows caused him to backpedal. The thought crossed my mind that he might be scared. Certainly he had to be shocked. He stumbled and I plowed into him, knocking him to the floor.

In a trance, I stood waiting. Nothing seemed real. The noise level was deafening. Two kids helped Neal off the floor and pushed him toward me. Apparently, no longer shocked by my unexpected intensity, he stalked toward me. Above the din, Pudge urged, "Circle, Ned, circle. Like Sugar Ray, remember?" And I did just like we practiced. Neal swung, I ducked. He swung again. I stepped aside. I circled, he missed. In frustration, he tried to corral me but I ducked under his grasp and stood free. There in a sea of swarming, shouting faces I spotted Bluto screaming, "Clobber the punk, Neal. If you don't, I will."

I abandoned the duck and weave and attacked Neal with both arms flailing away. One wild swing landed squarely on his nose and blood spilled forth; the sight of it charged my frenzied attack. Blow after blow landed on Neal's face and pushed him ever backward. Something primal broke free in me—I could't stop. I was not only fighting Neal but, in my mind, Bluto and the other ninth-graders. And I wasn't fighting for myself, but for Ralph, the seventh-graders and slight-built kids everywhere.

Neal's face had turned fearful, like an overripe peach, from the many blows that had hit their marks. He covered his face with his arms, protecting himself from my furious onslaught. He wasn't fighting back. He staggered and crumpled to the floor. Not able to hit him, I kicked him hard in the stomach, first with one foot then with the other. Kids yelled, "Stop it! Break it up! It's over!"

Pudge grabbed me from behind, dragged me down the hall and into the lavatory, all the while surrounded by screaming kids. Pudge sat me down in a stall. My heart pounded like a locomotive as I strained to hear what he was saying. "Calm down, calm down. You're okay. It's over. You won."

I struggled to regain control of my madly thumping heart and heaving chest. After several minutes, somewhat calm, the enormity of it all hit me. I had fought Neal and didn't embarrass myself or get hurt, although my arms and hands throbbed with a stinging ache. "Pudge, am I hurt?"

"You don't look it. You should see Neal, though, he's a mess. You went loco." Pudge squatted down in front of me and laughed. "I don't know what got into you. You sure didn't get it from me. You were boxing great for awhile, then you went nuts. I can't imagine anyone wanting to tangle with you, not even Bluto."

The mere mention of his name exhausted me further. "Bluto? I can't even run now."

"Calm down. Let's go to study hall. You gotta show up, know what I mean?"

I followed him to the auditorium where I was greeted with shouts of, "Way to go, Sugar Ned," and "Slugger," and, "Champion of Marshall High."

Nancy Harkness and Carole Clarke put their arms around me. Carole kissed me on the cheek and Nancy mockingly swooned, "My hero." I quickly slipped into a seat, opened a notebook and pretended to read. Fortunately, Mr. Watkins came in and quieted the place down.

I couldn't get over the commotion I'd caused. Maybe because kids didn't like Neal. Maybe because I was the underdog. More than anything, I couldn't get over *what* I'd done. I'd fought like a tiger loosed from its cage. I didn't understand any more than Pudge what had got into me. Maybe my weekend training gave me confidence. But I'd never hit anybody like that. Where did it come from? It was like a dream, and I was the tough guy for once. Maybe there was a little Bluto in me that I held in check because of my size. If I was bigger, maybe I'd be like him, too. Maybe everybody has a little Bluto in them.

The bell rang and the commotion started up again. Ralph shook my tender hand and said, "I saw the whole thing. You were super. Guess Bluto got to you and you took it out on Neal, huh?"

"I don't know, I just don't know."

"Maybe they'll stop messing with us seventh graders, whaddya think?"

Before I could answer, Pudge grabbed my arm and whispered in my ear, "C'mon, let's go home. We're going out the front door."

"Oh, garbage, now I gotta deal with Bluto."

Kids followed us down the corridor and out the front door. They probably thought there'd be another fight. I looked over to the side and, there by the fence where they usually hung out, stood Bluto and the other ninth graders. I held my breath, and tried to look away. Bluto just stared and the others nodded. After we passed them I said out of the corner of my mouth, "Pudge! Did you see that? Bluto didn't say a word. And, I swear, some of the guys nodded, like they were saying *nice job.*

"I don't get it. Bluto could still beat me to a pulp anytime he wanted to."

Pudge slapped my behind and grinned. "Yeah, but you just might get in a couple good licks, mess him up, know what I mean. Imagine kids laughing at him after you bloodied his nose. He knows you're going to fight back...and that makes all the difference in the world."

"Wow! Looks like I'm not a pushover anymore."

"You got it, Sugar."

"What a day! I can't wait for gym class on Thursday."

§ § §

DELIVERY BOY

"Can I have a dollar, Mother?" I yelled above the whine of the vacuum cleaner. "There's a super double feature at the Riverside Theater tonight—*Son of Frankenstein* and *House of Dracula.*"

"You know the rules, Ned," she shouted back. "A dollar a week and that's it."

"Can I have next week's allowance this week?" I countered.

"No." She turned off the Hoover. "If you need money, get a job. You know I don't make enough money to pay for your galavanting around town."

I goofed. I shouldn't have asked for a dollar just then. She was never in a good mood when she cleaned house. I braced myself for what was sure to come next.

Hands on hips, strands of graying hair dangling in front of her flushed but still pretty face, she fronted me as I lounged side-saddle across the living room chair. "Now, I don't ask you to pay room and board, all I ask is that you pay for your cokes, movies and all that other junk." She straightened her back, half turning away and choked, "I've told you a thousand times, I can't afford to pay for your foolishness."

"But Mother..."

"Don't *but* me," she ordered. "Why don't you get a job?" She shook her head. "No, no, that's *not* the *right* question." Her head bobbed from side-to-side, like she was looking for her car keys under the sofa cushions. "Why can't you keep a job? How many have you lost now? Answer me that?"

"You know how many," I replied. "Four."

"Fired from four jobs and you're only fourteen years old next week. And why did you lose those jobs? Because you don't think," she said, punctuating each word with a nod of her head. "And can you tell me, who beside you—in the history of the world—has ever gotten fired as a paperboy."

She talked to me like I was a juvenile delinquent or something. To her it was a crime to make a mistake. She must've thought I lost jobs on purpose. I wanted those jobs. I hated scrounging for nickles and dimes for frozen custards and comic books. Oh, scabpicker! Why did I have to go and ask her for money *now*?

I was desperate to calm her down so I said, "Mother, will you please relax?" I swung my legs to the floor and sat up in my chair. "I've got a job interview downtown on Monday."

I had caught her by surprise. She looked at me sideways for half a minute while she fidgeted with her apron strings. "That's good. Why didn't you tell me this before?"

"I was afraid you'd be mad if I didn't get the job."

"What kind of job?" she asked, lowering her voice as she sat down on the sofa.

"They want someone to make deliveries, you know, a delivery boy."

"Well, just don't lose it. Do as you're told and think for a change."

Lose it. No way. With luck, I'd soon be back in the money and back in her good graces, too.

After school on Monday, I caught the bus downtown to the Claxton building, rode the elevator to the fifth floor and opened the door to Cantrell Stock Service. A grim-faced, stout woman with a tight hairdo stood behind a desk and examined me keenly.

"You the boy from Marshall High?" she demanded.

"Yes, Ma'am."

"They said you'd be here at three. It's three-thirty," she huffed, looking at her thick, black-strap watch. "Time is important in my business. And there's no room for mistakes in my business, either. One screw-up and you're finished. Is that understood?" She shifted the man-sized belt cinched around her middle, sat down behind her desk and motioned for me to sit in the chair next to the desk. "Your job is simple. Everyday before you come here, you stop at the Northern Ohio Stock Exchange on the seventh floor of the Security Building. Got that?"

I nodded.

"You pick up a bag marked Cantrell—it'll be on the receptionist's desk—sign for it and then hightail it over here. No stopping anywhere. The girls here will take the tally slips out of the bag, sort them and type up the day's results, just like they're doing now."

I had barely noticed the girls when I entered the room. I glanced in their direction. They smiled and continued typing. I grinned in return.

"Are you listening?" Mrs. Cantrell snapped.

"Yes Ma'am."

"Pay attention then. After you've run ninety copies on the mimeograph machine, you help the girls fold them, slip them into pre-marked envelopes and sort them into two bags. Then you'll deliver the bags, one to the Stock Exchange, and one to the Cleveland Bank Building on East Ninth. After that, you can go home."

She riveted me again with her machine-gun eyes and I promptly nodded.

"Good, you understand. Business people and bankers want to know stock trading results first thing in the morning, if not before they go home at night. So, both bags must be delivered by six o'clock. Most days we deliver by five-thirty, don't we girls?"

The girls looked up from their typing and nodded agreement.

"I give my girls top wages and you'll get the same. A dollar an hour for three hours work a day. Today, you watch, tomorrow you work. "Got that?" she said not really expecting an answer as she directed me to a corner to watch. I tried to keep my mind on what they were doing, but all I thought about was my good fortune.

A dollar an hour! Most kids would die to make that much money. How lucky could I get? I'd make more money than Pudge who had the longest *Cleveland Plain Dealer* paper route on the west side; buy my own lemon phosphates and *Three Musketeers*; see a movie every Friday night; and on Saturday nights, treat the gang to birchbeer floats at Winterhurst iceskating rink. I could even slip a few bucks to Mother for room and board.

"Ned! That's your name, right?" Mrs. Cantrell bellowed. "Are you paying attention? Well, let's go, then. I'll show you the delivery route."

I followed her from building to building, trailing at her heels like a puppy. At every turn she barked out a rule followed by her signature, "Got that?" My response never varied, "Yes, Ma'am." She reminded me of that old battle-axe in the Marx Brothers movies. I sorta wished I was Groucho, but at a buck an hour she could bark at me all she wanted.

The job turned out to be a kick. Whenever old lady Cantrell took a break, I'd throw spitballs at the girls and they'd return fire with paper clips and erasers. I imitated the old battle-axe to make them laugh. I'd pinch my face like I'd just bit into a lemon, slip a dust-mop cover on my head and bark, "You're behind, girls. Speed it up. We've got deliveries to make. Got that?"

One afternoon, in Cantrell's absence, I slipped into character, slid behind her desk, picked up the phone and pretended I was talking to one of the suppliers. "Where's my paper stock? My girls are sitting here idle. My business is suffering. Timeliness is next to godliness. Got that?"

Just as I finished, she opened the door. "What are you doing at my desk?"

"Uh, answering the phone, Mrs. Cantrell," I said, quickly handing her the phone. "The line's dead though."

"Hummph. Get back to your machine, pronto. One of the girls should answer the phone, not you."

It was a close call. Thank goodness I'd whipped the mop cover off my head in time. Otherwise, I'd be right back where I started—out of money and in dutch with mother.

The pickup and delivery part of the job was fun, too. The guard at the Bank Building, a spindle-legged guy named Jackson, called me by name, and often left his post in the lobby and rode up and down in the elevator with me. He looked more like a chimney sweep than a lobby guard, but I'd never met a friendlier older guy.

Things couldn't have been better. I had a fun job, a wallet full of green smackers and, best of all, a happy mother who bragged to the neighbors about her hard-working teenage son who paid for his upkeep.

The moment I opened the door Monday afternoon I knew something was wrong. The girls gazed down at their typewriter keyboards. The battle-axe was apologizing profusely into the phone.

Cantrell slammed the receiver down. "You bonehead!" she screamed at me. "Nobody at the Bank Building got Friday's stock results. I've been on the phone all day trying to keep my customers. What did you do with Friday's delivery?"

"I delivered it like always," I assured her.

"Then why don't they have it? What did you do with it," she said through clenched teeth, her crimson face and quivering cheek muscles six inches from mine.

"I went to the Stock Exchange first like I always do—"

"I know that!" she bellowed, knocking me back on my heels. Then, lowering her voice, as if she was a cop detective I'd seen in the movies. "What did you do when you got to the Bank Building?"

I started to speak but hesitated when I remembered what happened. "Oh, no," I gasped, "he didn't."

"Who didn't?"

"Jackson."

"Who, pray tell, is Jackson?" her voice rising with each word.

"He's the lobby guard at the Bank Building."

"So?"

"I gave him the bag of envelopes to take up to the ninth floor 'cause I was in a hurry." Before she could interrupt, I quickly added, "Jackson goes in the elevator with me every day to the ninth floor and walks me to the Prescott office. He knows where the bag goes."

"You mean you gave the bag to someone else? To this guard?"

"I trusted him. He said he'd take a load off my hands since he could see I was in a hurry."

"What was so important that you couldn't take the bag up yourself?"

"I don't remember," I lied. I wasn't about to tell her

about the movie I went to see over on the east side.

"How could you be so stupid?" she said, shaking her head. "Didn't you use your brain?"

She paced the office thwacking her flattened palms against her considerable thighs. I hung my head and waited for the inevitable.

"All right, I told you, one mistake and you're out. I meant it. So get out."

I stared at the floor.

She slapped the desk. "Didn't you hear me? You're fired. Get out of here."

I stumbled out of the office down the stairs with Cantrell's voice trailing behind me. "I can't believe it! Did you hear that, girls? He gave the bag of envelopes to a guard. A guard! Do you think a guard knows what to do with our envelopes?"

I ran all the way to the Bank Building and caught Jackson at his post next to the elevators. Nearly out of breath, I panted, "What did you do with the bag on Friday?"

He stared at me with that hang-dog look of his and finally said, "Uh, oh. I was afraid something might happen."

"What did you do with the bag?" I pleaded.

"Well," he slowly began. "After you gave it to me, the elevator stopped on the third floor and the bank president got on. He asked me to hail him a cab and have the driver wait for him."

"The ba-aa-agg! What happened to it?"

"I'm getting to that. On the way out to the street I put it on top of the lobby mail box. When I came back it was gone."

"Who took it?"

"Well, I'm pretty sure the mailman did. He probably took one look at the bag, figured it was mail and put it in his sack. I'll ask him tonight when he comes in."

"Forget it," I said in disgust. "It won't do any good now. I'm already fired."

"Fired?" Jackson repeated. "You mean you lost your job over it?"

"You got it. And you could be in trouble, too. Old lady Cantrell's probably calling the bank president right this minute. I told her I gave you the bag."

"You can't get fired over one little mistake. Look, I'll call her and tell her it was my fault."

"I told you, forget it," I said, shaking my head in disgust. "I'm fired. One mistake with that woman and it's over."

"I'm sorry, Ned. Believe me I am. You're a nice kid. I just didn't—"

"I know, I know, you just didn't think," I finished the sentence for him. "Well, so long, Jackson. I'm going to the Arcade Building for a coke before I head home. I gotta figure out what to tell Mother. Geez, she's gonna kill me. So long."

I plopped down on an empty stool at the Arcade soda fountain and ordered a vanilla coke. I looked at my sorry self in the mirror behind the bar and shook my head. Another job down the drain.

I felt a tap on my shoulder, swirled around, and, it was Jackson, all red-faced and out of breath. He looked so excited I thought he was going to explode at any moment. "I've got it!" he exclaimed, dumping the bag on the stool next to me. "The mailman came by just after you left. Now you can get your job back."

"Jackson, sit down, will you." He took the stool on the other side of me, his long legs draping to the floor. He stared at me, a wide-mouthed grin frozen on his face.

"Look, I'm happy you got the bag, okay, but it's too late. It's Friday's bag, it's—"

He interrupted me. "You can take the bag to Cantrell and tell her—"

"Jackson, please. Don't you understand?"

He handed me a green envelope. "Open it. Now, *you'll* understand. Go ahead, open it."

I raised the flap and parted the slit. "What's this? Money?" My mouth dropped. "I've never seen so much money, what's this...a thousand dollars? Where'd you get this?"

"In the bag. Read the note, will you."

I slipped out the note and read it. I still didn't get it. "What's this mean?"

"Cantrell's running a scam."

"Scam?"

"Here's how I figure it." Jackson stood at attention, his lanky frame simulating an exclamation point. "She's running a weekly game. The broker guys pick a price for one of the stocks, how it's going to finish the week, okay, and then put money down on that price. You pick up their bets early in the week, and then deliver the payoff on Friday. That's why Friday's bag is so important."

"But, I've never seen this envelope—"

"When you take the pickup bag back to Cantrell, who gets it first."

"Well, old lady Cantrell always goes through the bag before the girls start typing..."

"See? And I bet she's the last to look at them, right?"

"Right." I paused to let it sink in. "Oh, my goodness...it's gambling." I hesitated. "That's okay, isn't it?"

"Nope. It's illegal. Now do you see how you're going to get your job back?"

"I think so, maybe."

The next afternoon I stood across from the Claxton building with the bag behind my back. As soon as Cantrell's girls left, I slipped across the street, took the elevator to the fifth floor and stationed myself outside Cantrell's office. I heard a shuffling noise inside, took a deep breath, and swung the door open. I voiced the line Jackson and I had practiced together all afternoon. "I found the bag, Mrs. Cantrell."

Cantrell stood erect, her cheeks changing color before my very eyes. I heard the wall clock tick several times. She growled in a low, menacing voice, "What are you doing here." Her voice cracked on the "here." She didn't move a muscle. I stared at a spot on the wall. All of a sudden she erupted. "Give me the bag. Give it to me." She snatched the bag from my outstretched hand and slung it down on the desk and immediately rummaged around inside with both hands, throwing envelopes to the floor with abandon.

I sprung my next rehearsed line. "Is this the envelope you're looking for?" I held the green envelope against my chest, away from her snake-like reach.

"What are you doing you little trouble-maker, give me that envelope. Give it to me?" I didn't say anything. She bellowed, "GIVE ME THE ENVELOPE." I swore I heard the windows rattle above my blood-pounded ears.

It was time for my third well-rehearsed line. "If you give me my job back?" I said meekly.

Cantrell looked like a prison guard ready to pounce on a poor defenseless inmate. But she didn't charge, she didn't say a word. So far, things were going exactly like Jackson said they would. I chanced another repeat. "I'd like my job back, please. I promise, I won't tell a soul. My mother'll kill me if you don't give me my job—"

"All right, bonehead...I mean, Ned. Hand me the envelope."

I handed it over. She counted the money faster than a bank teller on payday. "All here. Who else has seen the bag, the envelope."

"Nobody. The bag was tucked in a broom closet at the Bank Building. Jackson...the lobby guard...called me at home and told me to come pick it up. He didn't open it. He just gave me the bag." I paused. It was time for the clincher. "I knew what the envelope was immediately...I run numbers for my uncle over on the east side."

Dead silence. I dared not blink. Finally, she said, "Well, you never know, do you?" I thought I saw a smile, certainly I heard a chuckle. "You can have your job back, but not a word to anyone. No one, understand." She turned away, then shot back over her shoulder, "Got that?"

"Got that, Mrs. Cantrell, got that."

§ § §

From **The Bike Race**: "That beautiful bike. That beautiful bike that was going to leave me in the dust on Saturday afternoon, with show-off Neal riding high on that raised, pointy English seat, hands off the handlebars, arms outstretched, and me trudging behind on my clunky, one gear, fat wheeled All-American Schwinn."

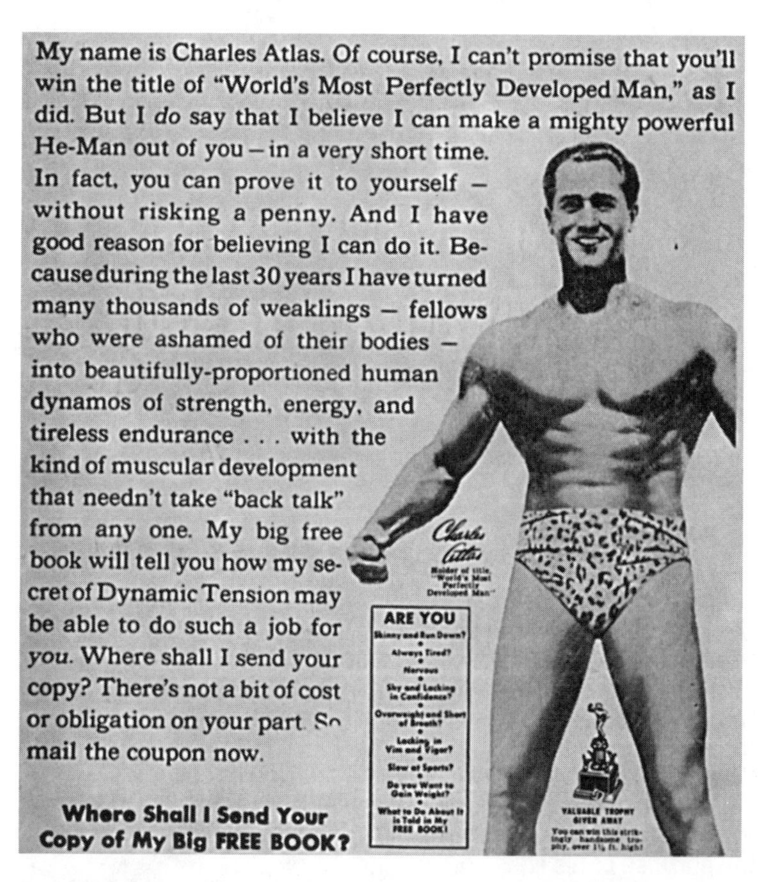

From **The Pushover**: "Pudge, I've been thinking. You lift weights and all. Maybe you could show me some things, like the *Charles Atlas* dynamic tension stuff." Pudge screwed up his face but I went on. "I'm tired of Bluto kicking sand in my face. I don't want to be a ninety-seven pound weakling all my life."

IM Press
P.O. Box 5346
Takoma Park, Maryland 20913-5346
301-587-1202
efaine@yahoo.com

Autographed and inscribed copies of this book can be **ordered** through **IM Press** at the above address. Send an $8 check (includes S&H) for each copy **ordered**.

The book can also be **ordered** through amazon.com.

And for those of you with kids or grandkids, check out the **LITTLE NED STORIES - Book One**, a chapter-picture book for kids 4-8 written by Edward Allan Faine, illustrated by Joan C. Waites.

Three separate stories describe the experiences of a six-year-old boy in West Virginia in the 1950s.

No Soap — Little Ned and Mr. Jenkins scour the West Virginia countryside in Mr. Jenkins truck looking for the "Man with the Money." They go to the blacksmith, the sawmill, the brickyard, the movie house, and the general store, and (okay, here's a secret) they find the "Man with the Money," but not before Little Ned finds something special: a brand new nickname.

The Boy Who Hated Halloween — Little Ned goes to a Halloween party in a strange town with Caspar the Ghost, Snow White, Pocahontas, Frankenstein and other monsters and gets the sur*prise* of his life!

The Ocean Vacation — Little Ned loves his nightly bath, loves the water, and wants to swim in the ocean, but not with spiders, snakes and goopy, slimy things. Well, boys and girls, find out how Little Ned overcomes his fear of the big blue endless ocean and learns how to swim.

Order **LITTLE NED STORIES** as above. Send $11 to IM Press (includes S&H). Don't forget to specify inscription, "To Samantha on her seventh birthday."